BlueberryMouse

by Alice Low

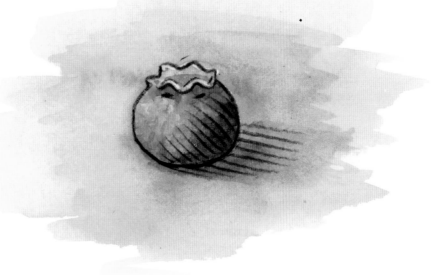

Illustrated by David Michael Friend

For Hannah and Isaiah—A.L.
To Ma and Pa, without whom my life would belong to another—D.M.F.

For information contact:
MONDO Publishing
980 Avenue of the Americas
New York, NY 10018
Visit our web site at http://www.mondopub.com

Printed in China
04 05 06 07 08 09 10 HC 9 8 7 6 5 4 3 2
04 05 06 07 08 09 10 PB 9 8 7 6 5 4 3 2 1

ISBN 1-59336-111-4 (hardcover) 1-59336-112-2 (pbk.)

Designed by David Michael Friend

Library of Congress Cataloging-in-Publication Data

Low, Alice.
Blueberry Mouse / by Alice Low ; illustrated by David Michael Friend.
p. cm.
Summary: Blueberry Mouse is convinced that a blueberry pie is the best place to live,
especially when she runs out of berries and begins to nibble the floor and walls.
ISBN 1-59336-111-4 (hc) - ISBN 1-59336-112-2 (pbk.)
[1. Mice--Fiction. 2. Dwellings--Fiction. 3. Blueberries--Fiction. 4. Pies--Fiction. 5.
Stories in rhyme] I. Friend, David Michael 1975-ill II. Title.

PZ8.3.L946B1 2004
[E]--dc22   2003059682

2

Out in Blueberry Cove,
On the Isle of Skye,
Lived the Blueberry Mouse,
In her blueberry pie.

When the other mice shouted,
"Hooray for blue cheese!"
She said, "Let them eat cheese,
I'll have blueberries, please."

4

Singing, "Blueberry, blueberry,
Blueberry pie
Is the best kind of house
For a mouse, and here's why....

If it's raining and blowing
You won't get wet feet.
You can stay in your house
To find something to eat.

For whenever you feel
Like a nibble or bite,
You can nibble a blueberry
Morning or night."

Singing, "Nibble, I'll nibble
All night and all day.
There's nothing like blueberries,
I always say."

She was totally blue
From her head to her toes,
With those blueberry whiskers
Beside her blue nose.

She'd a blueberry table
And blueberry cup...
Well, she did, 'til the day
That she nibbled them up!

Singing, "Nibble, I'll nibble,
I'll nibble away.
There's nothing like blueberries,
I always say."

Next she nibbled her
Blueberry blanket and sheet.
"I can do without them.
I can turn up the heat."

When she'd eaten her bedclothes,
She ate up her bed.
"I can sleep on my
Blueberry floor now," she said.

So she slept on her
Blueberry floor for a night,
But she couldn't resist
Taking bite after bite.

When she'd eaten her floor,
She said, "My, that was good!
For a blueberry floor
Tastes much better than wood."

Singing, "Nibble, I'll nibble
My blueberry house.
It's the best kind of house
For a Blueberry Mouse."

When she'd eaten her windows,
She nibbled some more,
'Til she'd eaten up all
Of her blueberry door.

When she'd eaten her door,
She said, "My, that was small.
I will nibble some walls,
For I don't need them all."

"Just as long as I have
A strong roof overhead,
I'll be sheltered from rainstorms,"
That little mouse said.

Singing, "Nibble, I'll nibble,
I'll nibble a wall,
First one...and then two...
And then three...and then all."

And so what happened then?
Well, the roof crust fell down
With a PLOP that was heard
Out in Blueberry Town.

Little Blueberry Mouse
Wasn't hurt in the least
And invited her friends
To come join in the feast.

Then they said to her,
"Dear little Blueberry Mouse,
Tell us where will you live now
Without any house?"

"Why, I'll pick some more blueberries,
And I will make
A much, much better house
In a blueberry cake."

Singing, "Blueberry, blueberry,
Blueberry cake
Is the best kind of house
That a small mouse can make."